CONTENTS

NOT FOR THE PUBLIC TO KNOW
TOP SECRET
ZONE 13 FILES ONLY

4

THE STATION

The underground train stopped at a station. Scott looked up from the horror story he was reading. Earls Court.

'Good,' he thought. 'The next stop is mine.'

Two people got off the train. No one got on. Scott was now the only person in the carriage. The doors closed and the train started, clanking over the points. Outside, everything was dark as the train went into a tunnel.

He went on reading his book. After a minute or two the train came out of the tunnel. It stopped and the doors opened. Scott got up and stepped out on to the platform. He was still reading his book. He put the book in his pocket and looked around him.

This wasn't his station! He was standing on an old wooden platform. Dust and dirt were everywhere. The station building had great holes in its roof. There was a dead, rotten smell in the air.

Scott turned quickly to get back on the train, but the doors had closed. The train didn't move. It just vanished!

Scott staggered back. What was going on? Where was the train? Why were the rails rusty and covered in weeds? Why was there a skeleton on the track?

And why was its grinning face staring at Scott?

FOOTSTEPS

Scott turned back to the station building. He had to get out of here! The door had fallen off its hinges. Beside it lay a pile of rags. Scott shuddered as he realized that it was a body. Bones were sticking out of the cloth, and a cloud of flies buzzed up as he passed.

Scott stepped out into the street. It was empty and silent. It was getting dark, but the streetlights weren't working. They were all smashed.

It looked like a city after a battle. A row of shops all had broken windows. All sorts of goods were thrown about. Cars rusted by the side of the road. Some of them had the remains of people inside. Further along the street a tall building was burnt black.

As Scott turned to walk down the street, he kicked something that skidded across the pavement. It was a gold coin. Nearby there were two more coins. They looked valuable. Scott picked them up and put them in his pocket.

He didn't know which way to go. He turned right into another street. It was getting darker now.

After a short distance, he stopped. He was sure he could hear footsteps behind him! He turned round, but he couldn't see anyone.

He carried on. The footsteps behind started again, louder and nearer now. He spun round. Still no one!

In a panic, Scott turned to run, but his way was blocked. Dark figures stood in a line across the road. They looked human, but their faces were missing. They wore dark hoods and long, dark cloaks. There was just a black hole where their faces should have been.

He turned again. There were more of them behind him! He was surrounded!

With a hissing laugh, the dark figures closed in on Scott.

TOP SECRET

ZONE 13 FILES ONLY

NOT FOR THE PUBLIC TO KNOW

THE RATS

Scott looked round wildly. He saw a dark alley between two buildings. Maybe he could escape that way. He rushed down it. He tripped on something on the ground. He put his hands out to save himself. He screamed out loud when he felt bones cracking under his hands.

He got up quickly and ran on. It was difficult to see where he was going. He didn't know if the strange figures were still chasing him.

He came out into another street. There was a shop opposite with its door open. Scott dived in. He thought he might find a place to hide.

It had been a small supermarket. The shelves were empty. There was a skeleton sitting at the checkout. It looked as if it had been waiting a very long time for customers.

Scott felt his way to the back of the shop.

Suddenly, he stepped into thin air. Stairs! He hadn't seen them in the darkness. He tried to save himself but the stairs were steep. He crashed to the bottom.

Scott felt bruised, but luckily he hadn't broken any bones. He sat up, groaning. He put his hand down to the floor.

He felt something soft moving under his hand.

The cellar was full of rats!

The smell was terrible. The soft, furry creatures had run away when he fell down the stairs. Now they started to jump all over him. They squeaked in the darkness.

He yelled and waved his arms, but the rats weren't frightened now. One of them bit Scott on the leg.

Now he knew why the bodies in the street were just bones. The rats had picked them clean – and he was fresh meat!

NOT FOR THE PUBLIC TO KNOW

TOP SECRET

ZONE 13 FILES ONLY

MEN WITH NO FACES

Scott struggled to his feet. A faint light came from the top of the stairs. This helped him find them. He started to climb up. The rats did not want to lose their meal. They clung on to his clothes with their sharp teeth.

At last Scott reached the top. There was still some light in the street. He rushed to the shop door. Behind him, he could hear the rats pouring out of the cellar. He could hear the

sound of their feet on the bare floor of the shop.

Shaking off the last rat, Scott burst into the street.

The dark figures with no faces were waiting for him.

There was no escape. There were more of them now, and they stood in a circle round him. Even the rats seemed afraid of them. They had followed Scott out of the shop, but now they all rushed back to their dark cellar.

'What do you want?' yelled Scott. 'Get away from me!'

But the figures just laughed, and closed in on him.

One of the figures was standing in front of him. Scott could see something under its hood. It had no face, but Scott could see eyes! They floated in the darkness.

As Scott watched, the eyes got brighter and brighter. They glowed yellow.

Scott reached out to push the figure away.

His arm passed straight through its body!

They weren't solid. They couldn't hold him. He rushed at the nearest figure. He would run right through it!

The strange, faceless creature held out his arms. He looked like a huge, black bat in the darkness.

As Scott passed through the figure, everything went completely dark. He could hear nothing and see nothing.

Then he did hear something. It was a faint squealing sound. It got louder and louder. Scott knew that sound. He had heard it many times before.

NOTHING BUT DUST

Scott was back on the train!

He looked round. There weren't many passengers in the carriage, and none of them looked weird in any way. They were just reading their papers or looking bored, wanting to get home.

With a squeal of brakes, the train stopped at the station. The doors opened. Feeling shaky, Scott looked out of the train window before he got off. He breathed a sigh of relief.

West Brompton! His station! Everything seemed normal.

He stepped off the train. The doors closed behind him and the train pulled out. It was evening, and the station was brightly lit. One or two other passengers had got off the train, and they were pushing their tickets into the ticket barrier and disappearing into the night.

Scott shook his head. Had it been real? Had he dreamt it? He couldn't have been dreaming! It was much too real, and he had been wide awake all the time! Perhaps he had been reading too many of those horror stories!

His book of horror stories was still in his pocket. He took it out and threw it into the rubbish bin.

Then Scott found something else in his pocket. He put his hand in and pulled out three golden coins. They were the ones he had found in the frightening world he had visited!

Then he noticed something. The coins had been bright and shiny, but now they were dull. He could feel them crumbling in his hands. He dropped them onto the platform. They broke into pieces.

Soon there was nothing but dust, scattering in the breeze that blew along the platform.

NOT FOR THE PUBLIC TO KNOW
TOP SECRET
ZONE 13 FILES ONLY

ABOUT THE AUTHOR

David Orme is an expert on strange, unexplained events. For his protection (and yours) we cannot show a photograph of him.

David created the Zone 13 files to record the cases he studied. Some of these files really do involve aliens, but many do not. Aliens are not everywhere. Just in most places.

These stories are all taken from the Zone 13 files. They will not be here for long. Read them while you can.

But don't close your eyes when you go to sleep at night. **They** will be watching you.